First U.S. Edition 1991

Library of Congress Catalog Card Number 90-53309

ISBN 0-316-37284-6

10 9 8 7 6 5 4 3 2 1

Printed in Italy

# MOUSE &
# Elephant

## by Matthias Hoppe
## Illustrated by Jan Lenica

 Little, Brown and Company
Boston   Toronto   London

Nicole the mouse had almost everything she needed to be happy.
She lived in a beautiful house with a lovely view. She had nice neighbors.
And she was very smart. But Nicole wasn't happy, because she was missing
something very important. Nicole didn't have a best friend.

All alone, she took a walk in the country, where she met a frog.

"Would you like to be my friend?" Nicole asked the spotted green stranger.

"Oh, no," said the frog. "I can only be friends with those who jump and croak like me." And with that, the frog leaped into the pond and was gone.

Nicole walked on until she ran into a caterpillar on stilts.
"Would you be my friend?" she asked.
"Oh, no," said the caterpillar. "I'm much too busy preparing

for the stilt-walking contest. You can't walk on stilts, can you?"
Without waiting for Nicole to answer, the caterpillar crashed
through the tall grass and was gone.

Then Nicole came to a place where a mole was working.
"Would you like to be my friend?" Nicole asked politely.
"You can't work hard like me," the mole said gruffly, "and
I'm much too busy to stand around and chat with someone as
small as you. Excuse me." And the mole disappeared down
one of the tunnels he was digging.

Nicole still had no friend of her own. She felt lonely enough to talk to a cat.

"Could you be my friend?" Nicole asked.

The cat's green eyes glowed. "Are you crazy? Cats and mice are enemies. We are too different to be friends. Everyone knows that. Now scram, before I eat you up!"

Frightened, Nicole scampered into the forest.  There she heard a very strange sound.  She looked around and saw a stag, who was singing. Nicole waited until he finished his song.

"Nobody will be my friend —" she began.

But the stag interrupted her. "Can you sing as wonderfully as I?"

Nicole shook her head no.

"Well, then, why should I be friends with someone as untalented as you?" the stag said.  Then he began to sing in a very loud voice and paid no more attention to the little mouse.

Nicole grew discouraged. No one wanted to be her friend. But she decided to keep trying.  She walked on in the woods. Soon she met a fat bear licking honey.

"Will you be my friend?" Nicole asked in a small voice.

"Do you like honey?" the bear asked Nicole.

"No, I don't," she replied.

"Well, how can I be friends with someone who doesn't like what I like?" the bear asked, as he turned away and gobbled up his honey greedily. Nicole hung her head and trudged away.

Nicole was sad. Would she ever find someone who would be her friend? Nicole walked out of the forest and found herself in front of a circus. She was surprised to see a huge elephant there, balancing on a stand. He was so big that he scared Nicole, but, drawing up her courage, she asked bravely, "Would you be my friend?"

"Friend? Friend? What is a friend?" the elephant asked. "I've never heard of such a thing."

"Well," Nicole replied, thinking hard, "I think a friend is somebody you can count on. Friends tell each other their feelings. Friends stick together and help each other."

The elephant thought a while and said, "That sounds good. I don't have anyone like that."

Surprised by the elephant's answer, Nicole said, "But I'm not like you at all! I can't balance on a stand, and I'm not very strong. And I'm much smaller than you are. Aren't we too different to be friends?"

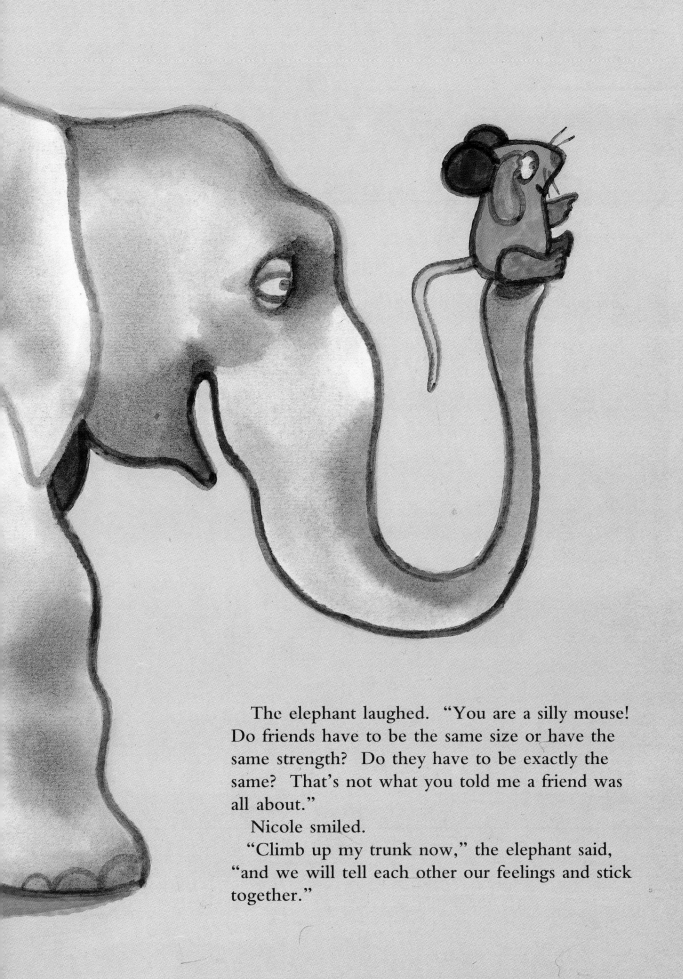

The elephant laughed. "You are a silly mouse! Do friends have to be the same size or have the same strength? Do they have to be exactly the same? That's not what you told me a friend was all about."

Nicole smiled.

"Climb up my trunk now," the elephant said, "and we will tell each other our feelings and stick together."

Off they went, and began to learn to be friends. The other animals knew nothing of this friendship. They were too busy thinking only of themselves.

But Nicole and the elephant knew. And each day as they visited and talked, they became better and better friends, even though one of them was very small and the other very big.